Published by Ladybird Books Ltd.,
80 Strand, London WC2R 0RL
A Penguin Company
Penguin Books Australia Ltd., Camberwell, Victoria, Australia
Penguin Books (NZ) Ltd., Private Bag 102902, NSMC, Auckland, New Zealand

2 4 6 8 10 9 7 5 3 1

Printed in Singapore

www.ladybird.co.uk

CLASSIC

Jungle Book

Ladybird

Deep in the jungle, a dark shadow slipped along silently through the undergrowth. He moved so softly that not a leaf stirred as he passed. It could only be Bagheera, the sleek black panther.

Suddenly Bagheera lifted his head to listen. He had heard a strange little cry in the distance. It came from somewhere near the river. Bagheera came to a half-sunken boat, and there, inside, was a baby boy lying in a basket.

"Why, it's a Man-cub!" Then he thought, I can't leave him here. He needs food and a mother's care. The panther picked up the basket gently and laid it on the bank.

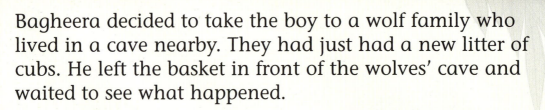

Bagheera decided to take the boy to a wolf family who lived in a cave nearby. They had just had a new litter of cubs. He left the basket in front of the wolves' cave and waited to see what happened.

When the baby cried some wolf cubs and their mother raced over to the basket. The she-wolf smiled when she saw the baby. "Oh, it's a Man-cub!" she said. "Poor little thing. If no one looks after him, he will die. I will have to look after him myself."

Bagheera was pleased. The Man-cub was going to be all right. He had been accepted into the wolf family. The mother wolf called him Mowgli.

Now, ten times the yearly rains had come and gone.
Mowgli had grown into a strong boy. He loved his family,
and Bagheera was one of his great friends. No one was ever
happier in the jungle than Mowgli.

Then one day, news spread that Shere Khan, the tiger, was back after a long absence. Akela, the leader of the wolves, called a meeting about it on Council Rock. Bagheera was there as well.

"When Shere Khan hears there is a Man-cub here," said Akela, "he will kill the boy and anyone who tries to protect him. For the safety of the pack, the Man-cub must go."

Bagheera had been listening closely. "The Man-cub could not survive alone in the jungle," he said. "But I can take him to a Man-village where he'll be safe."

"So be it," said Akela. "Go now. You've no time to lose."

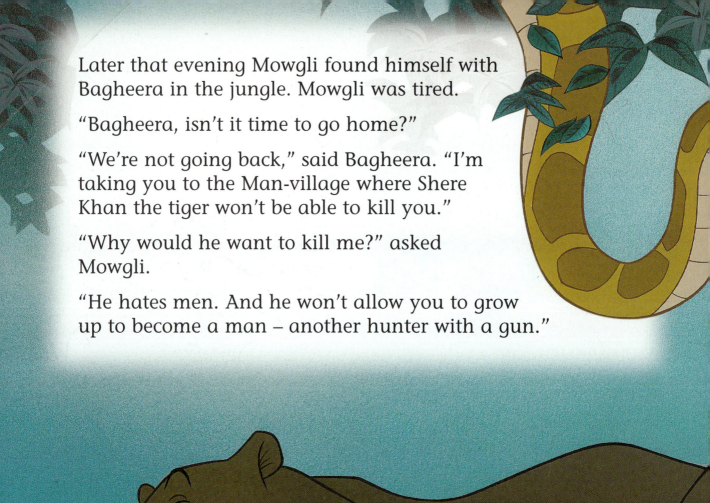

Later that evening Mowgli found himself with Bagheera in the jungle. Mowgli was tired.

"Bagheera, isn't it time to go home?"

"We're not going back," said Bagheera. "I'm taking you to the Man-village where Shere Khan the tiger won't be able to kill you."

"Why would he want to kill me?" asked Mowgli.

"He hates men. And he won't allow you to grow up to become a man – another hunter with a gun."

At last Bagheera stopped beneath a big tree. "We'll be safe in this tree – we can spend the night here."

He climbed the tree, stretched out along a branch and went to sleep. Mowgli wished he was back home with his wolf mother. The idea of living in the Man-village made him unhappy. With a yawn he decided he wasn't going to go there, and soon he fell asleep.

A while later, Mowgli woke to find two yellow eyes looking down at him. It was Kaa the python!

Kaa could make any beast or boy fall under his spell. He spoke in a soft whisper. "Go to sleep, Man-cub. Go to sleep." Mowgli's eyes grew heavy. Then Kaa coiled his tail round Mowgli's body and began to squeeze.

Just at that moment Bagheera woke up and saw what was happening. He leapt forward and swiped Kaa on the head with his big paw. Soon Mowgli was free of Kaa's coils, he gave the snake a good push and Kaa fell to the ground.

When Kaa had gone, Bagheera said, "Let's rest now. We have a long journey tomorrow." He curled his tail round Mowgli and they both fell asleep.

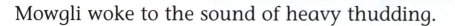

Mowgli woke to the sound of heavy thudding.

"Something's coming! Wake up, Bagheera," he cried. Bagheera put his paws over his ears and groaned. "Oh no, it's Colonel Hathi's Dawn Patrol!"

Mowgli climbed down to get a closer look. It was an amazing sight. A wrinkled old elephant was in the lead, behind him marched about a dozen sleepy elephants.

"Wake up!" cried the colonel.

Trailing along at the back, trying hard to keep up, was a baby elephant. Mowgli fell into step beside him.

"What are you all supposed to be doing?" he asked.

"Drilling, of course," the baby elephant replied proudly.

"May I join in?" asked Mowgli.

"Sure," said the baby elephant. "Just do what I do."

Mowgli got down on all fours and started to march along with the baby elephant. He could hear Colonel Hathi shouting, "Hup, two, three, four," at the head of the line.

"You see, it isn't really hard," said the baby elephant.

Then the colonel suddenly shouted, "Company, halt!"

The elephants stopped marching and stood in a row, ear to ear. The baby elephant took his place, with Mowgli beside him.

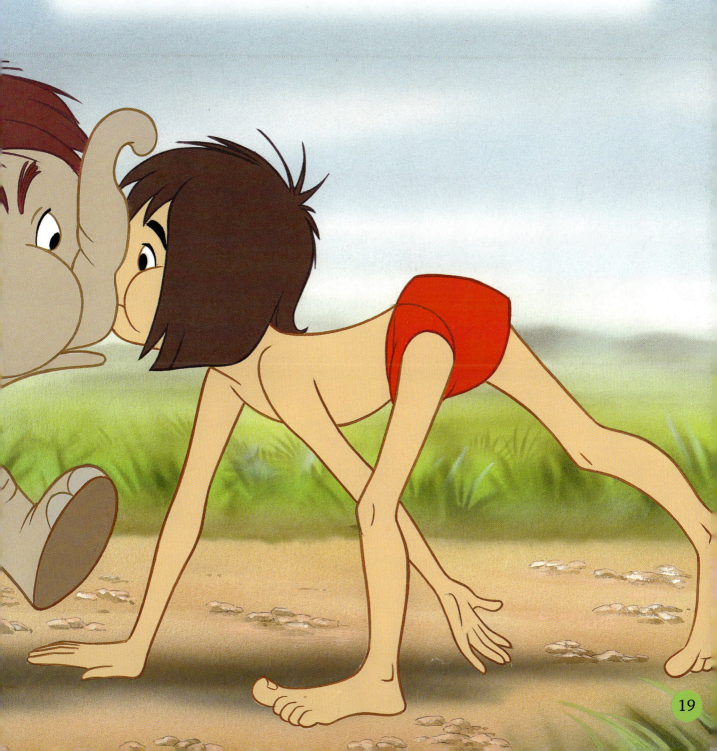

"Inspection!" cried the colonel.

All the elephants quickly raised their trunks.

Colonel Hathi inspected every elephant. None of them seemed to please him, although he smiled at the baby elephant. Then he came to Mowgli.

Colonel Hathi glared down at Mowgli, then picked him up in his trunk.

"What's this?" he cried. "A Man-cub? I'll have no Man-cub in my jungle!"

"It's not your jungle," said Mowgli, glaring back at him. "And you don't frighten me!"

That made the colonel even more annoyed, and he plonked Mowgli down beside the baby elephant.

Before Mowgli could guess what was going to happen next, Bagheera bounded up. He had heard everything.

"I can explain, Colonel Hathi," he said. "The Man-cub is with me. I'm taking him to the Man-village."

"But I don't want to go to the Man-village. I'm staying right here!" said Mowgli clinging to a nearby tree. Bagheera could not pull him off and he lost patience.

"Stay here, then. From now on, you're on your own."
With that, he turned and disappeared.

Mowgli was alone. "I can take care of myself," he said
bravely.

Then suddenly, he wasn't alone any more. He heard someone
singing and Baloo the bear came dancing towards him. Soon
they were friends.

Baloo taught Mowgli lots of things. "Bears never go hungry," he said. "Nature has provided everything we need. All we have to do is look."

Baloo and Mowgli danced happily as the bear showed Mowgli how to get honey from the bees and bananas from the trees.

"Mmm, great!" said Mowgli.

When they came to the river, Baloo jumped in and floated on his back. Laughing happily, Mowgli hopped onto the bear's stomach and snuggled close. They drifted peacefully along, knowing nothing of the mischievous monkeys who were following them from the trees.

Hanging by his tail, a big monkey suddenly swooped down and grabbed Mowgli.

"Take your hands off my cub," Baloo shouted, but the monkeys just laughed.

"Only the black panther can help me now," Baloo said to himself, and set off to find Bagheera in the jungle.

Fortunately, he was quite near. He listened to Baloo's story, then said, "They must have taken him to the ancient ruins, where the king of the monkeys lives."

The monkeys took Mowgli to a huge ruined temple. And there, seated on a stone throne, was King Louie. He smiled when he saw Mowgli. "So you're the Man-cub," he said. "Let's be friends."

One of the monkeys began to tap out a rhythm on a tree trunk, and the others began to dance and sing. In spite of himself, Mowgli was soon singing and dancing along with them.

"This is fun," he said.

"Yeah, ain't it?" said King Louie. "Now all I need from you, Man-cub, is the secret of Man's red fire."

"But I don't know how to make fire," said Mowgli.

Baloo and Bagheera had reached the ruins and were hidden close by. They could hear everything.

"Man's red fire! So that's what this is all about," gasped Bagheera. "We must rescue Mowgli quickly."

"What are we going to do?" asked Baloo.

"You create a disturbance and I'll rescue the Man-cub."

Shortly after, a big female monkey sidled right up to King Louie and started dancing. It was Baloo in disguise!

Louie was so taken by the big female that he didn't notice Bagheera creeping along the edge of the ruins, hoping to get near Mowgli.

As the music grew louder, the fun grew faster and more furious. Baloo was leaping around so much that his disguise slipped off. King Louie stared at him in surprise. "It's Baloo the bear!" he yelled.

When Mowgli heard that, he looked round and saw his friend. He ran up and jumped straight into Baloo's arms. The monkeys started to chatter angrily.

A tug of war began, with Mowgli caught in the middle. One minute Baloo had Mowgli, the next minute King Louie snatched him away.

"Please let me go!" begged Mowgli.

Then Bagheera came bounding to the rescue, with his claws out and his big teeth gleaming.

The monkeys were no match for the big panther. Frightened, King Louie let go of Mowgli. The three friends wasted no time leaving the ruined temple and the monkeys who lived there.

Later that night, Baloo, Bagheera and Mowgli rested on an island in the middle of the river. Mowgli went to sleep first, on a bed of soft leaves. As soon as he was asleep, Bagheera turned to Baloo, "Sooner or later, Mowgli's going to meet Shere Khan... "

"What's he got against Mowgli?" asked Baloo.

"He hates Man, and fears Man's fire. He wants to get Mowgli while he's young and helpless," Bagheera replied. "Someone the boy trusts must take him to the Man-village. And that means you."

"Come on, little man! Wake up! We're leaving," said the bear, gently shaking Mowgli awake.

"Already?" said Mowgli. "But where are we going?"

"A long way," Baloo replied sadly.

They turned and waved to Bagheera as they set off. "Good luck, Mowgli!" he called.

From time to time, as the two walked on, Mowgli asked, "Where are you taking me, Baloo?" And each time, his friend said nothing. At last Baloo had to confess, "I've promised Bagheera that I will take you to… "

He wasn't allowed to finish. Mowgli ran off into the jungle shouting, "Traitor! You're as bad as the others."

Mowgli was more unhappy than he had ever been in his whole life. He sat on a stone thinking sadly, "I have no friends left. There is no one in this jungle that I can trust anymore," he said.

"You must trust in me," slurred a slippery voice. Just then Kaa lifted Mowgli up into the trees. Kaa hyponotised Mowgli with his swirling eyes. He was soon in a trance. At this time, Shere Khan was passing under the tree.

He wondered who Kaa was talking to.

"I'd like a word with you if you don't mind," called Shere Khan.

Kaa quickly swooped his head down to see who was talking to him, he was careful to leave Mowgli on the branch of the tree. Khan didn't trust Kaa and Kaa didn't trust Khan.

The tiger thought that the wily python knew where Mowgli was but Kaa managed to persuade Khan that he knew nothing. When Shere Khan had gone the python lifted himself back up into the tree. Just then Mowgli snapped out of the trance. Frightened, he kicked Kaa out of the tree and ran away as fast as he could.

Mowgli ran and ran until he could run no more. Exhausted, he sat down on a rock. A storm was beginning to brew and the sky started to go very dark. Mowgli felt terribly alone.

A group of vultures were nearby, they had seen Mowgli arrive. One by one they flew down next to the Man-cub.

"Let's have some fun with this little fella. Legs like a stork but ain't got no feathers!" one of the vultures laughed.

"Go ahead, laugh! I don't care!" said Mowgli sadly.

The vultures felt very sorry for Mowgli.

"Poor little fella's down on his luck," said one of the birds.

The vultures told Mowgli that he could be an honorary vulture, Mowgli became a little happier. But there was danger nearby.

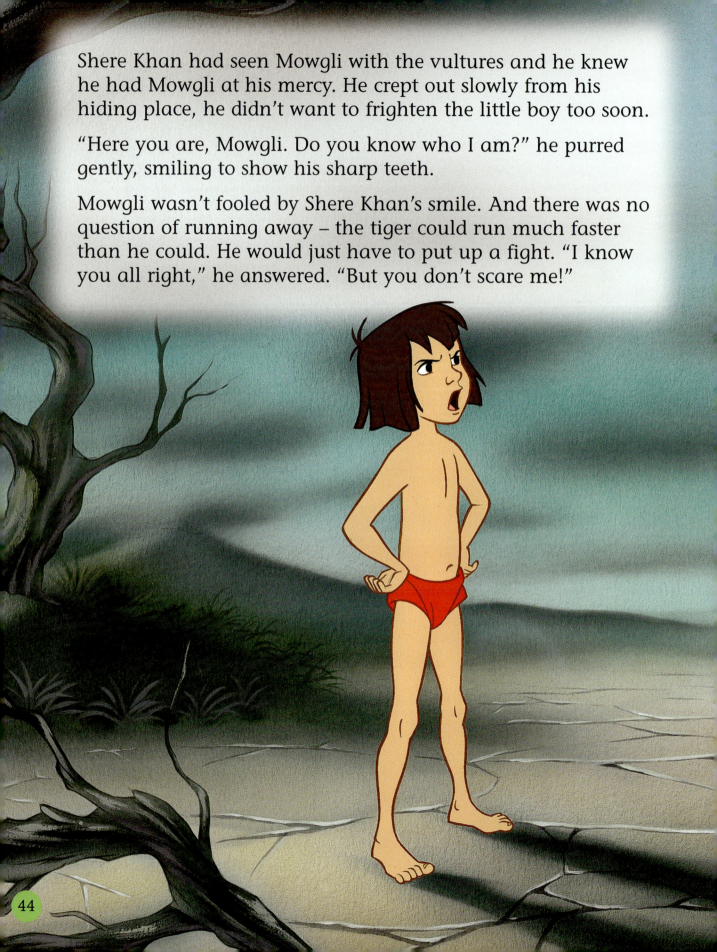

Shere Khan had seen Mowgli with the vultures and he knew he had Mowgli at his mercy. He crept out slowly from his hiding place, he didn't want to frighten the little boy too soon.

"Here you are, Mowgli. Do you know who I am?" he purred gently, smiling to show his sharp teeth.

Mowgli wasn't fooled by Shere Khan's smile. And there was no question of running away – the tiger could run much faster than he could. He would just have to put up a fight. "I know you all right," he answered. "But you don't scare me!"

"Ahhh," sighed Khan. "You have spirit. And for that you deserve a sporting chance." He smiled again. "You can try to escape, and I'll catch you. I'll close my eyes and count to ten. Ready? One, two, three, four... "

When Shere Khan got to ten, he opened his eyes. But instead of running away, Mowgli was still facing him.

"You don't scare me," he said again, and he grabbed a heavy branch and swung it at the tiger.

Shere Khan's smile had disappeared.

"That's it!" he said, furious that a tiny Man-cub had dared to attack him. "No more games!" He gave a fierce roar and bared his claws, ready to pounce. The little boy shrank back, terrified.

But some surprising help was at hand! Just as the tiger sprang at Mowgli, he stopped in mid air and crashed to the ground.

Someone had grabbed him by the tail to try to stop him! Baloo had turned up at the right moment once again, and was holding on to the tiger's tail with all his strength.

"Save yourself!" he yelled.

The vultures helped Mowgli get away from Shere Khan. As Mowgli looked back he realised that Baloo was in trouble. Mowgli had only one thought in his head – to go back to help his friend.

Baloo certainly was in trouble! Shere Khan had spun round, and with one powerful blow had knocked the bear over backwards.

Just as Baloo landed with a thud, a flash of lightning lit up the jungle.

Thunder crashed, and another streak of lightning set a tree ablaze. A burning branch fell at Mowgli's feet. Looking down at the fire he realised that he now had a real weapon – one that he knew the tiger feared.

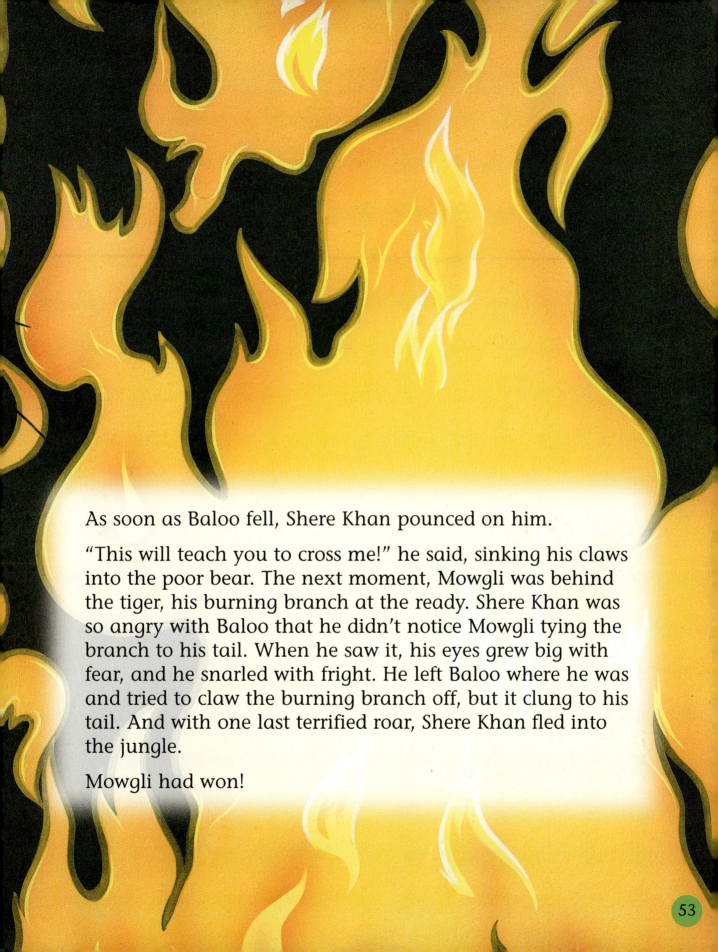

As soon as Baloo fell, Shere Khan pounced on him.

"This will teach you to cross me!" he said, sinking his claws into the poor bear. The next moment, Mowgli was behind the tiger, his burning branch at the ready. Shere Khan was so angry with Baloo that he didn't notice Mowgli tying the branch to his tail. When he saw it, his eyes grew big with fear, and he snarled with fright. He left Baloo where he was and tried to claw the burning branch off, but it clung to his tail. And with one last terrified roar, Shere Khan fled into the jungle.

Mowgli had won!

As Baloo was hugging Mowgli, Bagheera burst from the undergrowth just in time to see the fleeing tiger.

"Well done, Mowgli!" he cried.

"From now on, there will be nothing to stop you living in the jungle," said Baloo, very proud of his friend.

Bagheera sighed deeply. Whether he wanted to or not, Mowgli belonged to the Man-village. He defended himself in the same way that men did, not like an animal. Bagheera suddenly thought of a way to get him there.

"Since we've come so far, it would be a pity not to see what the Man-village looks like," he said cunningly.

Bagheera went on, "We can see it from the edge of the jungle."

"All right," said Mowgli.

And as he spoke, they heard someone singing. Then they saw that they were near some huts. "What's that?" asked Mowgli.

"Oh, that's the Man-village," replied Bagheera.

"No, I mean that," said Mowgli, pointing to a pretty little girl filling a jug with water from the river. It was she who had been singing. "I've never seen one before. I want to take a closer look," he said. "I'll be right back," he yelled as he made his way down a path.

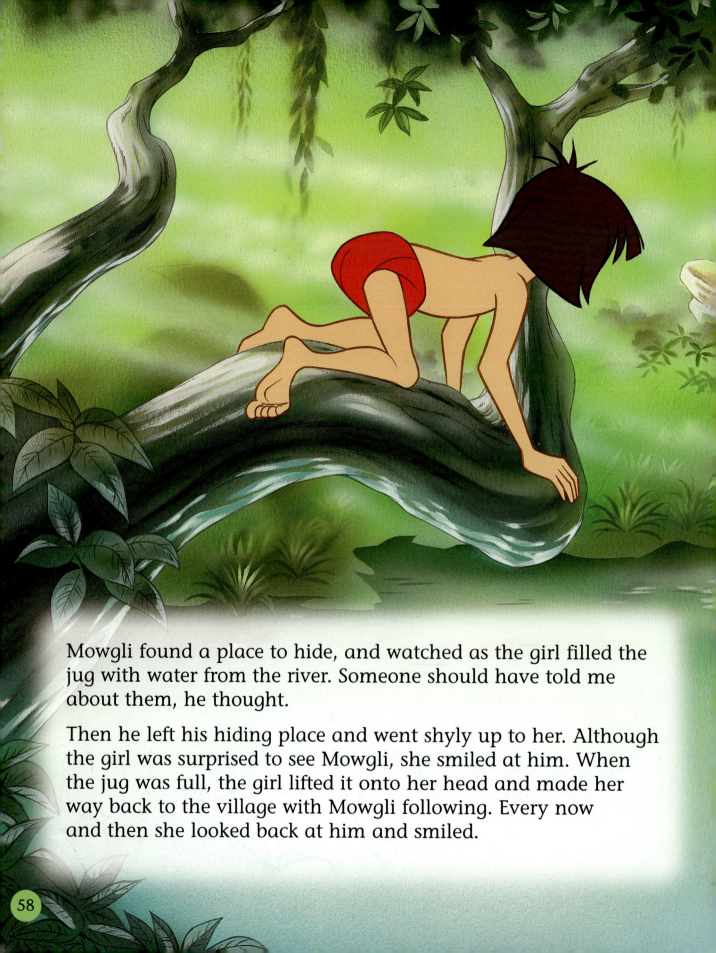

Mowgli found a place to hide, and watched as the girl filled the jug with water from the river. Someone should have told me about them, he thought.

Then he left his hiding place and went shyly up to her. Although the girl was surprised to see Mowgli, she smiled at him. When the jug was full, the girl lifted it onto her head and made her way back to the village with Mowgli following. Every now and then she looked back at him and smiled.

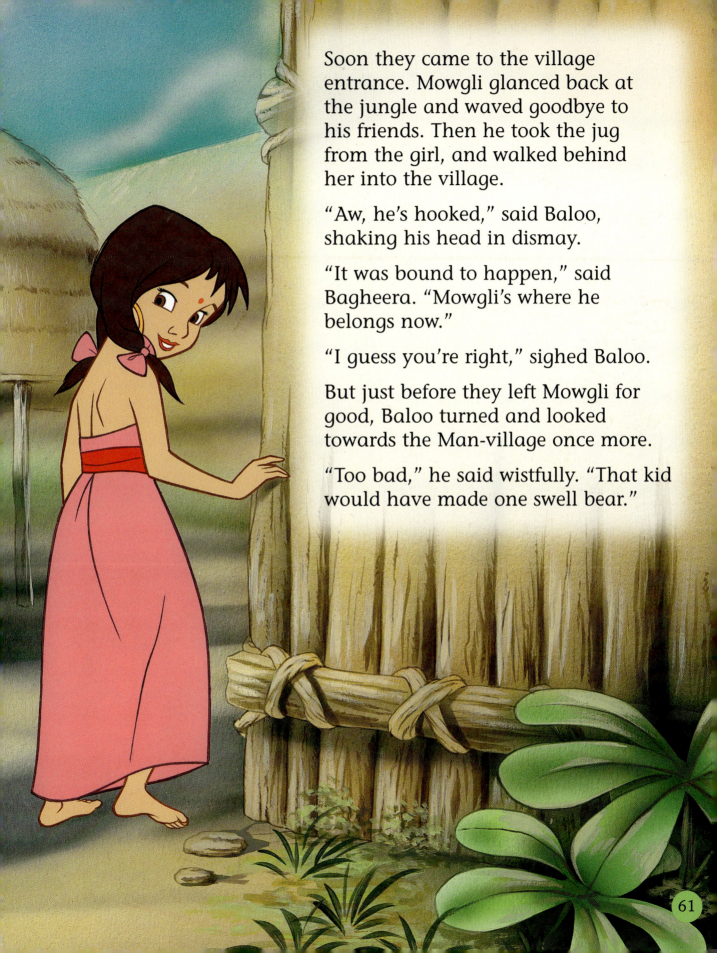

Soon they came to the village entrance. Mowgli glanced back at the jungle and waved goodbye to his friends. Then he took the jug from the girl, and walked behind her into the village.

"Aw, he's hooked," said Baloo, shaking his head in dismay.

"It was bound to happen," said Bagheera. "Mowgli's where he belongs now."

"I guess you're right," sighed Baloo.

But just before they left Mowgli for good, Baloo turned and looked towards the Man-village once more.

"Too bad," he said wistfully. "That kid would have made one swell bear."